A WOLF in the NORTH WOODS

Written by Heather Horn

Illustrated by Victoria Skakandi

goodandbeautiful.com
Cover design by Phillip Colhouer

Animals you will meet in the North Woods:

wolf (wolves)

bear

deer

eagle

moose

turkey

wild cat

rabbit

Challenge Words

berries

group

learn

turkeys

watch

world

CHAPTER 1

Pups in a Den

Will and Beth are two small newborn wolf pups.

They live in a warm den with their mother and father. The den is a small cave for the pups to stay safe and warm as they grow.

Their mother will keep them close and warm in the den until they are ready to go out and explore safely.

Will and Beth are so young that they have not left the den yet.

They also have four littermates, so there are six cute pups in the litter.

Mom licks her pups. The pups cannot walk yet, so they feel their way to Mom's belly to keep warm and find milk.

Will lets out a yip and Beth lets out a yap when the rest of the pups try to push up to Mom too. They all need milk from Mom.

They cannot see yet. Beth cannot open her eyes, and Will's eyes are shut too.

Since they are so young, they are both deaf and blind, so Mom helps them. When they crawl to their mother, she feeds them milk. It will be two weeks until they can see.

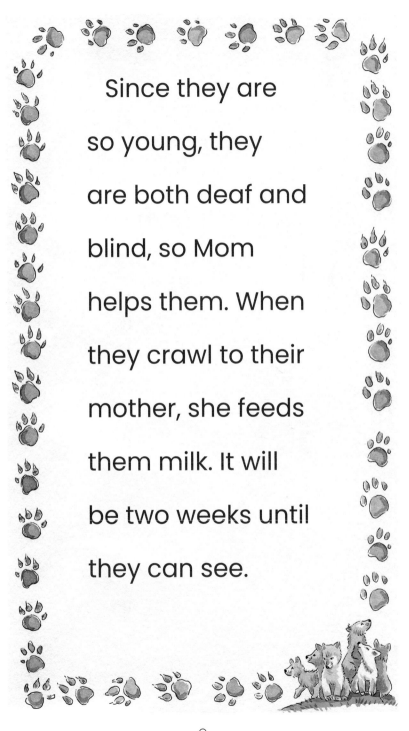

CHAPTER 2

Pups Can See

The pups are bigger and are fifteen days old.

Will and Beth have their blue eyes open, but they cannot see clearly yet. They have small teeth, but they still drink only milk from their mother.

The pups
stay in the
den with
Mom since
they are still
too small to
go out.

The pups are good littermates.

They play with paws and noses,

and sometimes they try to howl.

They are growing stronger.

It will not be long until they will

go out to run and play in the big

woods.

Mom needs food too, so Dad gets some for her and brings it back to the den.

CHAPTER 3

Pups Come Out

The pups are now four weeks old. Look how fast they have grown!

Beth and Will and the rest of the pups spent two months in Mom's tummy and one more month in the den.

Their den is safe, but it is time to see outside and look at the world around them.

Will gets up and takes a step out of the warm den. He sees the sun shining on the trees.

Beth steps out with Will. It is spring, and the land is waking up from the long winter.

The white snow has melted, and the trees are budding. The grass is soft on the pups' paws.

It is not long till Mom sees two of her pups are missing. She steps out from the den. The rest of the pups come too. There is so much for the small pups to see and smell.

Mom is close. Dad comes close to the pups too. If a bear sees them, the pups are at risk.

Dad keeps a lookout, and the small pups put each nose to the sky. Their ears perk up, and their noses wiggle. What is that?

They can smell now! The fresh
breeze and green grass smell
so sweet!

CHAPTER 4

Pups Eat Meat

The pups have more teeth now, so they are eating meat.

The wolf pack stays close and brings the food to the den, so Mom does not need to leave the pups. They are too small to hunt, so the pack will bring meat to them.

There are fifteen wolves in the pack who live and hunt side by side. Mom and Dad are the pack leaders. They tell the wolf pack the plan to hunt and find food to feed them all.

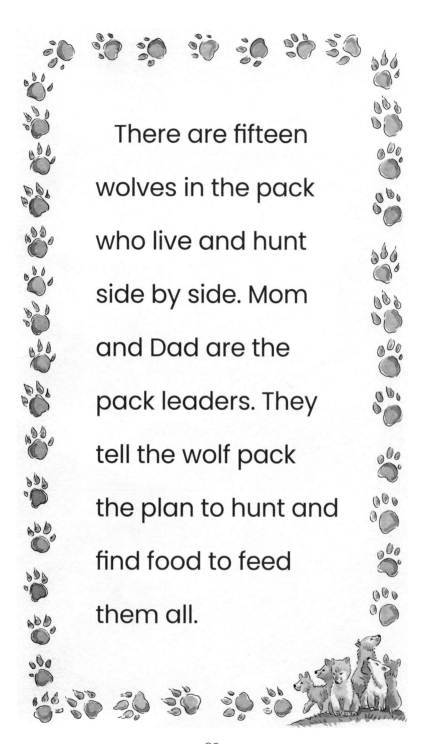

At dark they will hunt. The pack can see well in the dark and can creep up on animals.

Wolves have a soft step, and the deer in the woods do not hear them. The small pups will like this food.

After hunting that night, the
pack comes back to the den.

The pups lick the big wolf's mouth, and the wolf spits the meat up for the pups to eat. It is wolf baby food!

CHAPTER 5

Pups at Play

The next day the pups come out to play and enjoy the outdoors again.

They are getting brave, and they stay outside for a long time. The pack looks out for eagles in the blue sky.

The pups are small and still at risk, but they romp and roll in the open. This play is helping them grow strong.

Will sees a deer skin left from last night's hunt. Will and the other pups bat it back and forth.

Beth sees a bone and marches away with it in her lips. She is proud of her find.

This looks like play and is fun for the pups, but it is also helping them learn to hunt. They will need to hunt with their pack as they grow bigger and stronger.

In a short time, they will be able to hunt with the pack. For now, they learn to chat with yips, howls, growls, and looks.

They are learning to be part of the pack. It will soon be time for them to start hunting too.

CHAPTER 6
Pups Explore

Over the last weeks, the pups have learned a lot of things from their mother and father.

In the daytime they go out exploring with the pack. They look closely with their eyes and sniff the air. Deep in the woods, the pack sees a moose drinking from the pond.

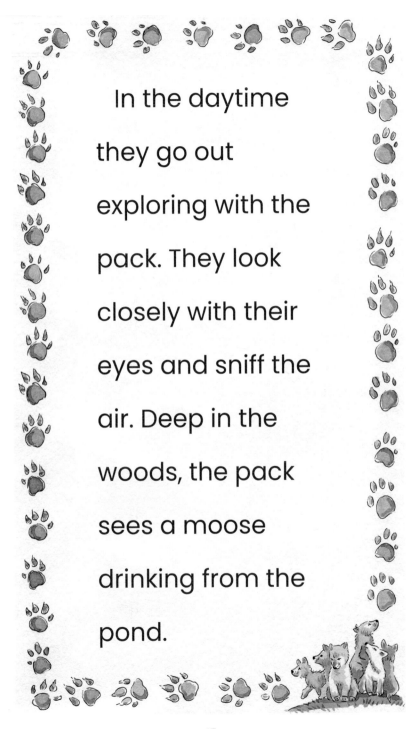

His long legs make him tall, so he bends his long neck to get a drink.

The pack hides in the trees. It is not yet time for any of them to hunt.

The pack walks on and sees a group of wild turkeys, called a "rafter." They are pecking at the stones and grass for bugs to eat. At first they do not see the pack.

In the bushes the wolves find sweet, ripe berries. Crunch! One of the pups steps on a stick. The turkeys hear the pups and rush off. They do not want to be dinner for the pack!

The pack moves on past a small brook. They stop for a cool drink. Beth looks in the water and sees herself.

She also sees
a fish and bats
it with her paw.
It swims away.
The pack calls
for her with a
bark: "Let's go!"

Next, the pack comes to a rocky hill. The big wolves stay close to the pups since wild cats will be looking, and the pups will not be safe. Dad barks and growls as he sees a cat on the hill. This is how he scares the big cat away and warns the pack of danger.

The pack barks too. The strong cat jumps from rock to rock, keeping watch.

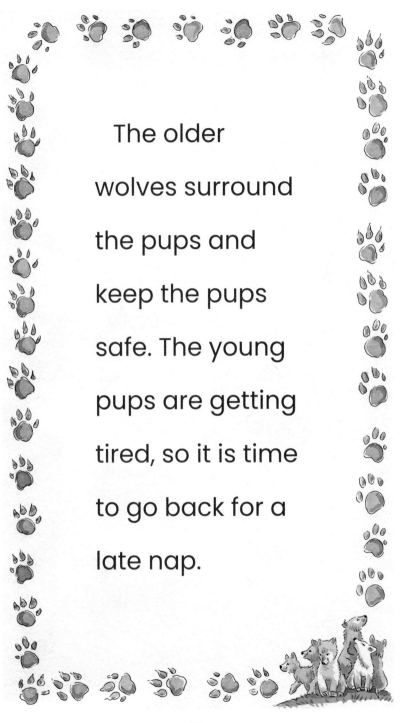

The older wolves surround the pups and keep the pups safe. The young pups are getting tired, so it is time to go back for a late nap.

CHAPTER 7

Pups Hunt

The summer sun is setting in the west. The pups are waking from the late rest. For Will, Beth, and the rest of the pups, tonight will be their first time hunting.

The big wolves start to howl and sniff. The small pups do the same. They are happy to join the hunt.

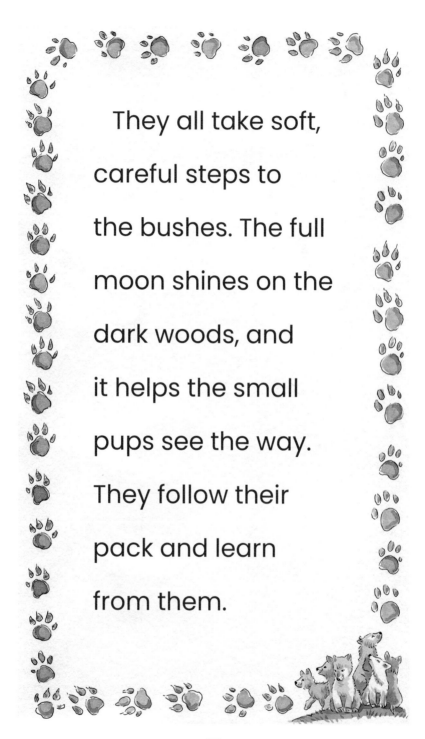

They all take soft, careful steps to the bushes. The full moon shines on the dark woods, and it helps the small pups see the way. They follow their pack and learn from them.

In the tall bushes on a hill, they hear a rustle. Rabbits smell the pack and are hiding within.

Some rabbits hop out the
back side, but two rabbits meet
Will and Beth. The pups grab
them with their sharp teeth.

The pups have had a good first hunt. It is sad for the rabbits, but it is part of life. If the pups did not eat, they would not live.

God gives all
the animals
open land to
live on, to grow,
and to be free.
Sometimes
wolves do not
get the rabbits,
and sometimes
they do.

From the largest animal to the smallest, God takes care of them all. When the sun comes up, it will be a new day.

It will be a new day for the pack and a new day for all the animals of the North Woods.

More Level 2A books from
The Good and the Beautiful

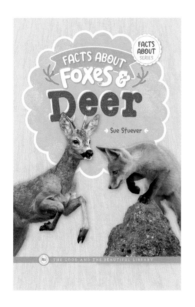

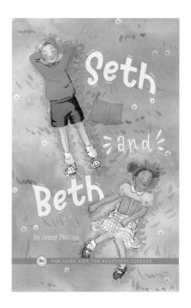

Facts About Foxes & Deer
By Sue Stuever

Seth and Beth
By Jenny Phillips

goodandbeautiful.com